Dear Parent:

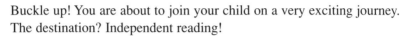

Buckle up! You are about to join your child on a very exciting journey. The destination? Independent reading!

Road to Reading will help you and your child get there. The program offers books at five levels, or Miles, that accompany children from their first attempts at reading to successfully reading on their own. Each Mile is paved with engaging stories and delightful artwork.

Getting Started
For children who know the alphabet and are eager to begin reading
• easy words • fun rhythms • big type • picture clues

Reading With Help
For children who recognize some words and sound out others with help
• short sentences • pattern stories • simple plotlines

Reading On Your Own
For children who are ready to read easy stories by themselves
• longer sentences • more complex plotlines • easy dialogue

First Chapter Books
For children who want to take the plunge into chapter books
• bite-size chapters • short paragraphs • full-color art

Chapter Books
For children who are comfortable reading independently
• longer chapters • occasional black-and-white illustrations

There's no need to hurry through the Miles. Road to Reading is designed without age or grade levels. Children can progress at their own speed, developing confidence and pride in their reading ability no matter what their age or grade.

So sit back and enjoy the ride—every Mile of the way!

A GOLDEN BOOK • New York
Golden Books Publishing Company, Inc. New York, New York 10106

ISBN: 0-307-26306-1   A MCMXCVIII

Barbie™

barbie.com:
the first adventure

by Barbara Richards
illustrated by S.I. International

Amy and Michelle were best friends.

They loved to play video games.

They loved to draw pictures

with their glitter pens.

But most of all,

they loved to play

with their Barbie dolls.

One day Amy went

to Michelle's house.

"Let's play school," said Michelle.

"Barbie will be the teacher."

"I wish she could be our teacher

next year," said Amy.

Michelle put her arm around her friend.

At school their teacher had told them

some bad news.

Next year there would be two

fourth-grade classes.

Michelle and Amy would not be together.

"What will we do without each other?"

cried Amy.

"Let's not worry about that now,"

said Michelle.

"I have a great idea.

Let's check out the new Barbie website.

Barbie will cheer us up."

The two girls went into the family room.

Marshmallow was asleep

on top of the computer.

Marshmallow was Michelle's fat cat.

"Maybe Marshmallow can help us

find *barbie.com*," giggled Amy.

Michelle picked up the cat.

"The only thing Marshmallow can find

lately is her food dish," she groaned.

"Should I ask my mom to help us

get online?"

"No," said Amy.

"We know how to use the computer."

Amy turned on the computer.

She typed *barbie.com*.

The screen turned bright pink.

A picture began to form.

"This is so cool!" cried Amy.

A window appeared.

Michelle read aloud,

"To take a virtual tour

of Barbie's house, click here."

She clicked the mouse.

But nothing happened.

"Let me try," Amy said.

She began clicking the mouse.

CLICK! CLICK! CLICK!

Suddenly, the door to Barbie's house

swung open!

A tiny voice called out,

"Hello, Amy and Michelle!"

Amy and Michelle leaned closer

to the computer.

"M-m-maybe I should get my mom,"

Michelle stammered.

"Wait a minute," Amy said.

"Let's see what happens next."

Words flashed across the screen.

Amy read,

"If you want to take

a *real* tour of Barbie's house,

click here."

Amy and Michelle stared at each other.

Was this really happening?

Amy clicked the mouse.

The screen began to flash.

Light pink! Hot pink! Cotton-candy pink!

Marshmallow hid under the desk.

Amy read the words on the screen.

"Do you really want to go?"

it asked.

"Do we?" Michelle laughed.

Amy giggled.

She pressed Enter.

A picture of a room appeared.

There was a computer in the corner.

"It's Barbie's room!" cried Michelle.

And then, something strange happened.

The computer screen began to grow.

It grew so large

that Michelle and Amy

stepped right into the screen!

Pink fog swirled around them.

A voice called out, "Welcome!"

Michelle and Amy blinked hard.

It was Barbie!

"You girls said you would like

to visit, right?" Barbie asked.

Michelle grabbed Amy's hand.

"You bet!" they both said.

"Okay," said Barbie, smiling.

"I just need to print out these flyers.

I'm organizing a fashion show.

We want to raise money

to feed hungry children.

I'll be ready in a few minutes."

Barbie's room had two big bookcases.

Michelle read some

of the book titles:

Windsurfing. Ice Dancing. Scuba Diving.

"Wow, Barbie really likes sports!" she said.

Amy pointed to a framed picture

on the wall.

It showed Barbie with her arm

around a huge elephant.

"You said it!" Amy agreed.

"Here's Barbie on a safari in Africa!"

Amy picked up a statue of a dog.

She read, "Barbie, Volunteer of the Year."

"That statue is from the animal shelter,"

Barbie explained.

She placed the flyers in a pink box.

"I love to take care of animals,"

Barbie said.

"Do you girls have any pets?"

Michelle nodded.

"I have a cat named Marshmallow,"

she said.

"And Amy has a dog named Goldy."

"How would you two like to see

one of my most special pets?"

Barbie asked.

Michelle and Amy looked at each other.

They were very excited.

"Let's go!" Amy shouted.

Barbie led the girls outside to the stable.

A brown horse with a yellow mane

poked his head out.

"This is Nibbles," said Barbie.

Amy patted the horse's mane.

"Can I feed him, Barbie?" she asked.

Barbie pulled an apple out of her pocket.

She handed it to Amy.

Amy fed Nibbles the apple.

"Amy loves horses," Michelle told Barbie.

"I can see that," Barbie laughed.

Amy could not stop smiling.

She patted the horse's mane.

"What a good horse," she said.

Nibbles put his head on Amy's shoulder.

"He likes me!" Amy squealed.

"So, Michelle, what do you like to do?"

asked Barbie.

"Michelle is a really great pitcher,"

said Amy.

"Really?" said Barbie.

"Oh, sure," said Amy.

"She's the best softball player

in our whole school."

Barbie thought for a moment.

"Well, we don't have enough

players for a whole game,

but we can still play catch."

"That would be great!"

yelled Michelle.

Barbie, Amy, and Michelle played catch.

Soon, it started getting dark.

"Someday you two

will have to come visit again.

I will gather some friends

together for a game,"

said Barbie.

Amy smiled.

"We would love to come back," she said.

"Great," said Barbie.

"But now, it's time for a treat."

They all went to Barbie's kitchen.

"How would you each like

a strawberry smoothie?" asked Barbie.

"Yummy!" said Amy and Michelle.

"Amy and I love strawberry smoothies,"

said Michelle.

Barbie put some fruit into the blender.

"You two must be best friends," she said.

"Just like me and my best friend, Midge.

We grew up together.

And we were always in the same class

at school."

"That does sound like us," said Amy.

"But next year will be different."

Barbie turned off the blender.

"How will it be different?" she asked.

Michelle told Barbie about the two

fourth-grade classes.

"It's not fair!" Michelle complained.

"We're best friends.

Best friends should always be together."

Barbie poured the smoothies

into three tall glasses.

"Let me tell you a story," she said.

"It's about best friends."

"One year Midge's family decided

to move to another town," said Barbie.

"I felt so sad.

I didn't want Midge to leave.

She was my best friend.

What would I do without her?"

Michelle and Amy leaned closer.

"What did you do, Barbie?" they asked.

"Midge and I wrote letters

to each other," said Barbie.

"We talked on the phone.

And I even got to visit her

in her new town.

Today we are still best friends."

"We can talk on the phone," said Amy.

"And we can see each other at lunch,"

said Michelle.

"Or after school!" yelled Amy.

"And don't forget weekends,"

added Michelle.

Barbie smiled.

"A best friend is always with you," she said.

"She is with you in your heart."

Michelle and Amy grinned at each other.

"Thanks, Barbie," they said.

Soon it was time to go.

"Can you help us get home?"

Michelle asked Barbie.

"Sure," said Barbie.

"Follow me."

Barbie led the girls back

to the computer room.

She turned on the computer.

She typed in the words,

michelle.com.

The screen began to flash pink.

Before long,

a picture of a room appeared.

"My computer room!"

cried Michelle.

Barbie's computer screen began to grow.

The girls hugged Barbie good-bye.

"Come visit me again," said Barbie.

"We will!" said Michelle and Amy.

Then they stepped through the screen.

"That was so cool!" said Michelle.

They were back

in Michelle's family room.

"No one will believe us," said Amy.

"Then it will be our secret,"

said Michelle.

Amy grinned.

"One best friends' secret coming up!"

she said.

They shook pinkies.

Suddenly, Marshmallow jumped

onto Michelle's lap.

She stared at the computer.

"I think your cat wants to visit Barbie,"

giggled Amy.

"Maybe someday she will,"

laughed Michelle.

"Maybe someday . . ."